THIS WALKER BOOK BELONGS TO:

_____

_____

_____

_____

My Cat

Patricia

WALKER BOOKS
AND SUBSIDIARIES
LONDON • BOSTON • SYDNEY

*For Les, Cliff, John, Colin, Amanda
and the cats at Wood Green Animal Shelter.*

First published 1994 by Walker Books Ltd
87 Vauxhall Walk, London SE11 5HJ

This edition published 1996

10 9 8 7 6 5 4 3 2

© 1994 Patricia Casey

Printed in Hong Kong

British Library Cataloguing in Publication Data
A catalogue record for this book is available
from the British Library

ISBN 0-7445-4360-6

Jack

Casey

My cat Jack is a

yawning cat.

He's a
stretching-down cat.

He's a
stretching-up cat.

My cat Jack is a scratching

cat.

He's a
curling cat.

He's a lapping

cat.

My cat Jack is
  a purring cat,
a rough-tongued cat,
  a washing cat.

He's a
cat who

likes washing
all over.

My cat Jack
is a playing cat.

He's a pouncing

cat.

He's an
acrobat cat.

And sometimes
he's a silly old cat.
I love him,
my cat Jack.

MORE WALKER PAPERBACKS
For You to Enjoy

WAG WAG WAG
by Peter Hansard/Barbara Firth

"Delightful… The text consists mainly of a small number of verbs
which very effectively portray the ups and downs and ins and outs of a canine day.
The illustrations are deceptively simple, vigorous and extremely appropriate."
Children's Books of the Year

0-7445-4736-9   £4.99

MOUSE PARTY
by Alan Durant/Sue Heap

"A simply rhymed, escalating book about a mouse
who throws a party for his odd friends…
Readers will want to rave on with this one until they drop."
The Observer

0-7445-4390-8   £4.50

THE OWL AND THE PUSSYCAT
by Edward Lear/Louise Voce

"One of the best-loved nonsense rhymes of all time…
The simple illustrations have an appealing charm – a picture book children will love."
Practical Parenting

0-7445-3121-7   £4.99

THE HUNGRY CAT
by Phyllis King

This tale of a cat who just can't stop eating is both
an exuberant counting book and an entertaining first reader.

"A wow with cat-lovers and cat-haters alike." *Rachel Anderson, Good Housekeeping*

0-7445-1415-0   £3.99

Walker Paperbacks are available from most booksellers, or by post from B.B.C.S., P.O. Box 941, Hull, North Humberside HU1 3YQ
24 hour telephone credit card line 01482 224626

To order, send: Title, author, ISBN number and price for each book ordered, your full name and address,
cheque or postal order payable to BBCS for the total amount and allow the following for postage and packing:
UK and BFPO: £1.00 for the first book, and 50p for each additional book to a maximum of £3.50.
Overseas and Eire: £2.00 for the first book, £1.00 for the second and 50p for each additional book.

Prices and availability are subject to change without notice.